THE COCK,

THE MOUSE

AND THE

LITTLE RED HEN

The COCK, *The* MOUSE
and the
LITTLE RED HEN

AN OLD TALE RETOLD
by
FÉLICITÉ LEFÈVRE

WITH 24 ILLUSTRATIONS
by
TONY SARG

E
Le

MACRAE · SMITH · COMPANY
PHILADELPHIA

To My Nieces

CECILIA GARRY and NELLY MELVILLE

AND

TO MY LITTLE FRIEND

HARFORD LURY

THIS BOOK IS DEDICATED

WITH MY LOVE

4 5 1 1

TWENTIETH PRINTING

Manufactured in the United States of America

THE COCK,

THE MOUSE

AND THE

LITTLE RED HEN

Once upon a time there was a hill, and on the hill there was a pretty little house.

It had one little green door, and four little windows with green shutters, and in it there lived

A Cock

and a Mouse

and a Little Red Hen.

On another hill close by
there was another little
house. It was very ugly.

It had a door that wouldn't shut, and two broken windows, and all the paint was off the shutters.

And in this house

there lived

A BOLD BAD FOX
and FOUR BAD
LITTLE FOXES.

One morning these
four bad little foxes

came to the

    big bad Fox and said:

"Oh, Father, we're so hungry!"

"We had nothing to eat yesterday," said one.

"And scarcely anything the day before," said another.

"And only half a chicken the day before that," said the third.

"And only two little ducks the day before that," said the fourth.

The big bad Fox shook
his head for a long time,
for he was thinking.

At last he said in a big gruff voice:

"On that hill over there I see a house. And in that house there lives a Cock."

"And a Mouse," screamed two of the little foxes.

"And a little Red Hen,"
screamed the other two.

"And they are nice and fat,"
went on the big bad Fox.
"This very day I'll take my
great sack and I will go up
that hill and in at that door,
and into my sack I will put
the Cock and the Mouse
and the little Red Hen."

"I'll make a fire
to roast the Cock,"
said one little fox.

"I'll put on the saucepan
to boil the Hen,"
said the second.

"And I'll get the frying pan to fry the Mouse," said the third.

"And I'll have the biggest helping when they are all cooked," said the fourth, who was the greediest of all.

So the four little foxes jumped for joy, and the big bad Fox went to get his sack ready to start upon his journey.

But what was happening to the Cock and the Mouse and the little Red Hen all this time?

Well, sad to say, the Cock and the Mouse had both got out of bed on the wrong side that morning.

The Cock said the day was too hot, and the Mouse grumbled because it was too cold.

They came grumbling down to the kitchen where the good little Red Hen, looking as bright as a sunbeam, was bustling about.

"Who'll get some sticks to light the fire with?" she asked.

"*I* shan't," said the Cock.

"*I* shan't," said the Mouse.

"Then I'll do it myself,"
said the little Red Hen.

So off she ran to get the
sticks.

"And now, who'll fill the kettle from the spring?" she asked.

"*I* shan't," said the Cock.

"*I* shan't, said the Mouse.

"Then I'll do it myself,"
said the little Red Hen.
And off she ran to fill
the kettle.

"And who'll get the breakfast ready?" she asked, as she put the kettle on to boil.

"*I* shan't," said
the Cock.

"*I* shan't," said
the Mouse.

"I'll do it myself," said
the little Red Hen.

All breakfast time the Cock and the Mouse quarrelled and grumbled. The Cock upset the milk jug, and the Mouse scattered crumbs upon the floor.

"Who'll clear away the breakfast?" asked the poor little Red Hen, hoping they would soon leave off being cross.

"*I* shan't," said the Cock.

"*I* shan't," said the Mouse.

"Then I'll do it myself," said the little Red Hen.

So she cleared everything away, swept up the crumbs, and brushed up the fireplace.

"And now, who'll help
me to make the beds?"

"*I* shan't," said the Cock.

"*I* shan't," said the Mouse.

"Then I'll do it myself," said the little Red Hen.

And she tripped away upstairs.

But the lazy Cock and Mouse each sat down in a comfortable armchair by the fire—

and soon

fell fast asleep.

Now the bad Fox had crept up the hill and into the garden, and if the Cock and Mouse hadn't been asleep they would have seen his sharp eyes peeping in at the window.

"Rat tat tat, Rat tat tat,"
the Fox knocked at the door.

"Who can that be?" said the Mouse, half opening his eyes.

"Go and look for yourself if you want to know," said the rude Cock.

"It's the postman perhaps," thought the Mouse to himself, "and he may have a letter for me." So without waiting to see who it was, he lifted the latch and opened the door.

As soon as he opened it
in jumped the big Fox, with
a cruel smile upon his face!

"Oh! oh! oh!" squeaked the Mouse as he tried to run up the chimney.

"Doodle doodle do!" screamed the Cock as he jumped on the back of the biggest armchair.

But the Fox only laughed, and without more ado he took the little Mouse by the tail and popped him into the sack, and then he seized the Cock by the neck and popped him in too.

Then the poor little Red Hen came running downstairs to see what all the noise was about—

and the Fox caught her
and put her into the sack
with the others.

Then he took a long piece of string out of his pocket, wound it round and round and round the mouth of the sack, and tied it very tight indeed.

After that he threw the sack over his back and set off down the hill.

"Oh! I wish I hadn't been so cross," said the Cock, as they went bumping about.

"Oh! I wish I hadn't been so lazy," said the Mouse, wiping his eyes with the tip of his tail.

"It's never too late to mend," said the little Red Hen. "And don't be too sad.

"See, here I have my little
work-bag, and in it there is
a pair of scissors and a
little thimble and a needle
and thread. Very soon you
will see what I am going
to do."

Now the sun was very hot, and soon Mr. Fox began to feel his sack was heavy, and at last he thought he would lie down under a tree and go to sleep for a little while.

So he threw the sack down with a big bump, and very soon fell fast asleep.

Snore, snore, snore went the Fox.

As soon as the little Red
Hen heard this, she took out
her scissors and began to
snip a hole in the sack, just
large enough for the Mouse
to creep through.

"Quick," she whispered to the Mouse, "run as fast as you can and bring back a stone just as large as yourself."

Out scampered the Mouse, and he soon came back dragging the stone after him.

"Push it in here," said the
little Red Hen, and he
pushed it in in a twinkling.

Then the little Red Hen snipped away the hole till it was large enough for the Cock to get through.

"Quick," she said, "run and get a stone as big as yourself."

Out flew the Cock, and he soon came back quite out of breath, with a big stone, which he pushed into the sack too.

Then the little Red Hen popped out, got a stone as big as herself, and pushed it in.

Next she put on her thimble, took out her needle and thread, and sewed up the hole as quickly as ever she could.

When it was done, the Cock and the Mouse and the little Red Hen ran home very fast, shut the door after them, drew the bolts, shut the shutters and drew down the blinds, and felt quite safe.

The bad Fox lay fast asleep under the tree for some time, but at last he woke up.

"Dear, dear," he said, rubbing his eyes and then looking at the long shadows on the grass, "how late it is getting. I must hurry home."

So the bad Fox went
grumbling and groaning
down the hill —

till he came

to the stream.

Splash! In went one foot. Splash! In went the other, but the stones in the sack were so heavy that at the very next step down tumbled Mr. Fox into a deep pool.

And then the fishes carried him off to their fairy caves and kept him a prisoner there, so he was never seen again.

And the four greedy little foxes had to go to bed without any supper.

But the Cock and the Mouse never grumbled again. They lit the fire, filled the kettle, laid the breakfast and did all the work, while the good little Red Hen had a holiday and sat resting in the big armchair.

No foxes ever troubled them again, and for all I know they are still living happily in the little house with the green door and green shutters, which stands on the hill.

The End

E
L
Lefevre, F. *C* /
The cock, the mouse
and the Little Red
Hen

	DATE DUE		